For all the children who care about
someone with dementia

Acknowledgements
With heartfelt thanks to Martin Slevin and Monday Books,
the author and publishers of *The Little Girl in the Radiator*.

Many of the events in this story are based on the actual events
that happened to Martin's mum and which are recorded
in his wonderful book.

First published in Great Britain and in the USA in 2019 by
Otter-Barry Books, Little Orchard, Burley Gate, Herefordshire, HR1 3QS
www.otterbarrybooks.com

ISBN 978-1-910959-94-7

Illustrated with mixed media

Printed in China

9 8 7 6 5 4 3 2 1

ME AND MRS MOON

HELEN BATE

Otter-Barry BOOKS

I'm Maisie.

Mrs Moon and Dylan are my best friends in all the world, and this story is about how important friends can be, and how they should always stick together whatever happens.

QUACK
QUACK
QUACK

QUACK
QUACK
QUACK

My friend, Mrs Moon, lived next door to me and my mum and dad. After school and in the holidays, she always looked after me and my friend Dylan.

It was like having another grandma, and we called her Granny Moon.

Granny Moon had a little dog called Jack. Most days after school we took him for a walk through the park on our way home.

In the school holidays, Granny Moon had loads of good ideas for things to do, so we were never bored. We really loved her looking after us.

If it rained, Granny Moon took us swimming... she was a fantastic swimmer.

My favourite time was when we all dressed up and Granny Moon took photographs of us with her old camera. We had one published in a magazine and we won first prize.

Sometimes, on rainy days, Granny Moon would go up into the loft and find boxes that all seemed to be full of interesting treasure.

Oh dear... NO!

AAGHH!

Even though we sometimes had accidents, Mum said she never worried about me when I was with Mrs Moon, because Mrs Moon used to be a nurse and always knew what to do.

To grandma love from Nathan xx

A Koala Bear

Ouch! It hurts.

...don't run about for a while. I'll get a box for you to sort out.

Look at this old penknife!

This is GORGEOUS.

The trouble started that November. Granny Moon was taking us to see a film as a surprise, but there was a problem with her new coat...

It's so cold today... I'd better wear my new coat.

But what's happened to the sleeves?? It looks like someone's cut them off...

OH NO! That must have been my sister Julia again. She's in BIG trouble this time! I'll tell Mum.

We'd never heard of Julia or Granny Moon's mum before... but we were late so Granny Moon put on another coat and we set off for the cinema.

Unfortunately the film was really very scary. Granny Moon must have forgotten about Dylan's fear of aliens and although I was OK, we had to leave early.

Oh dear... Dylan won't like this film... he'll be having nightmares again...

I think we'd better go.

What's the matter, Dylan?

Then, just before the Christmas holidays, even stranger things started happening next door.

One day, when we got back from school...

A man staggered in with the sort of Christmas tree that they usually put up in the town square. It was **massive!**

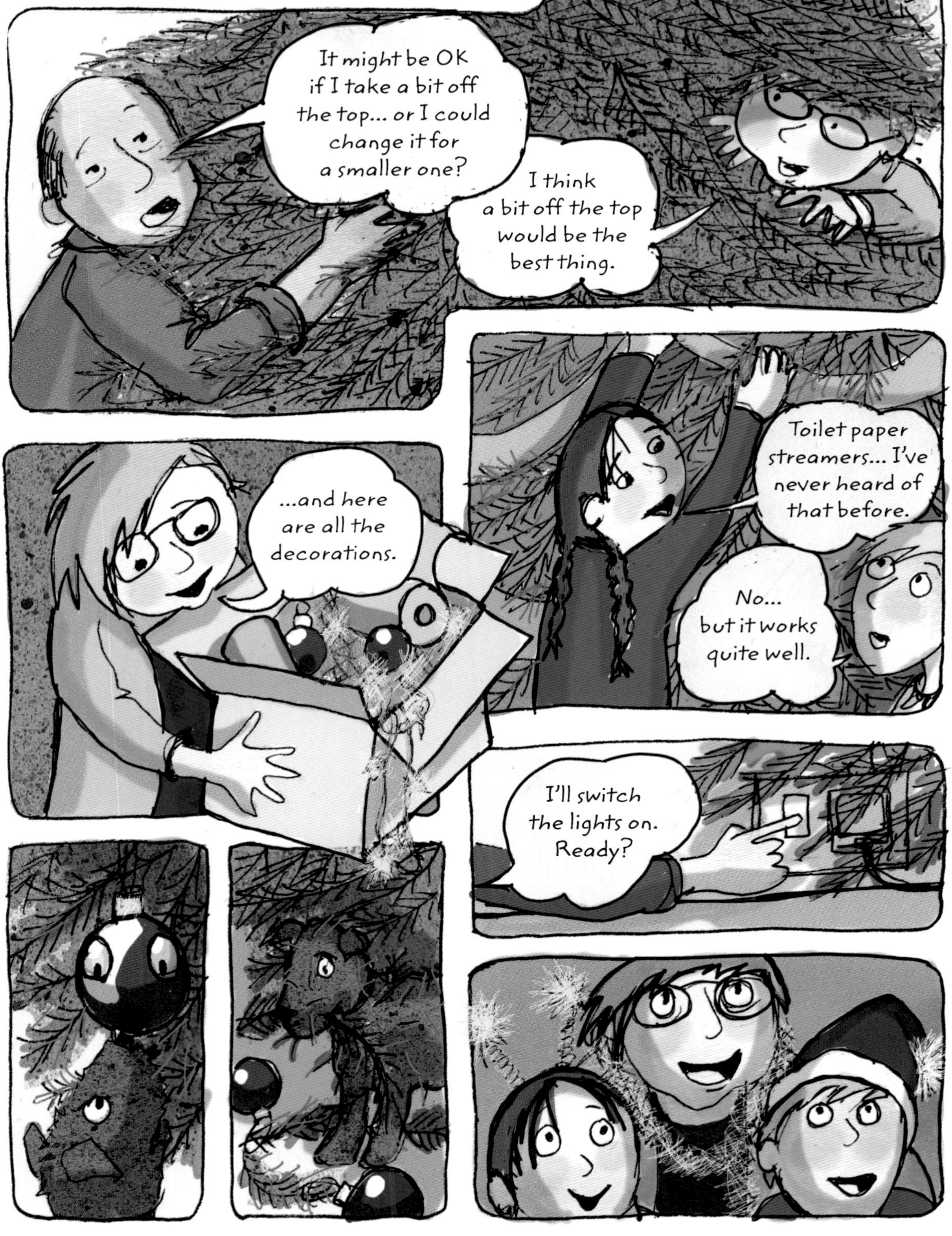
It might be OK if I take a bit off the top... or I could change it for a smaller one?
I think a bit off the top would be the best thing.
...and here are all the decorations.
Toilet paper streamers... I've never heard of that before.
No... but it works quite well.
I'll switch the lights on. Ready?

I was really happy that day, helping to put up the Christmas tree. I didn't know that tomorrow was going to be one of the most embarrassing days of our lives!

It started with everyone at school getting ready for the Christmas concert.

At last it was our turn to sing. My mum and dad couldn't be there, and nor could Dylan's, but Granny Moon was coming. We were really excited – but when the curtains were drawn back...

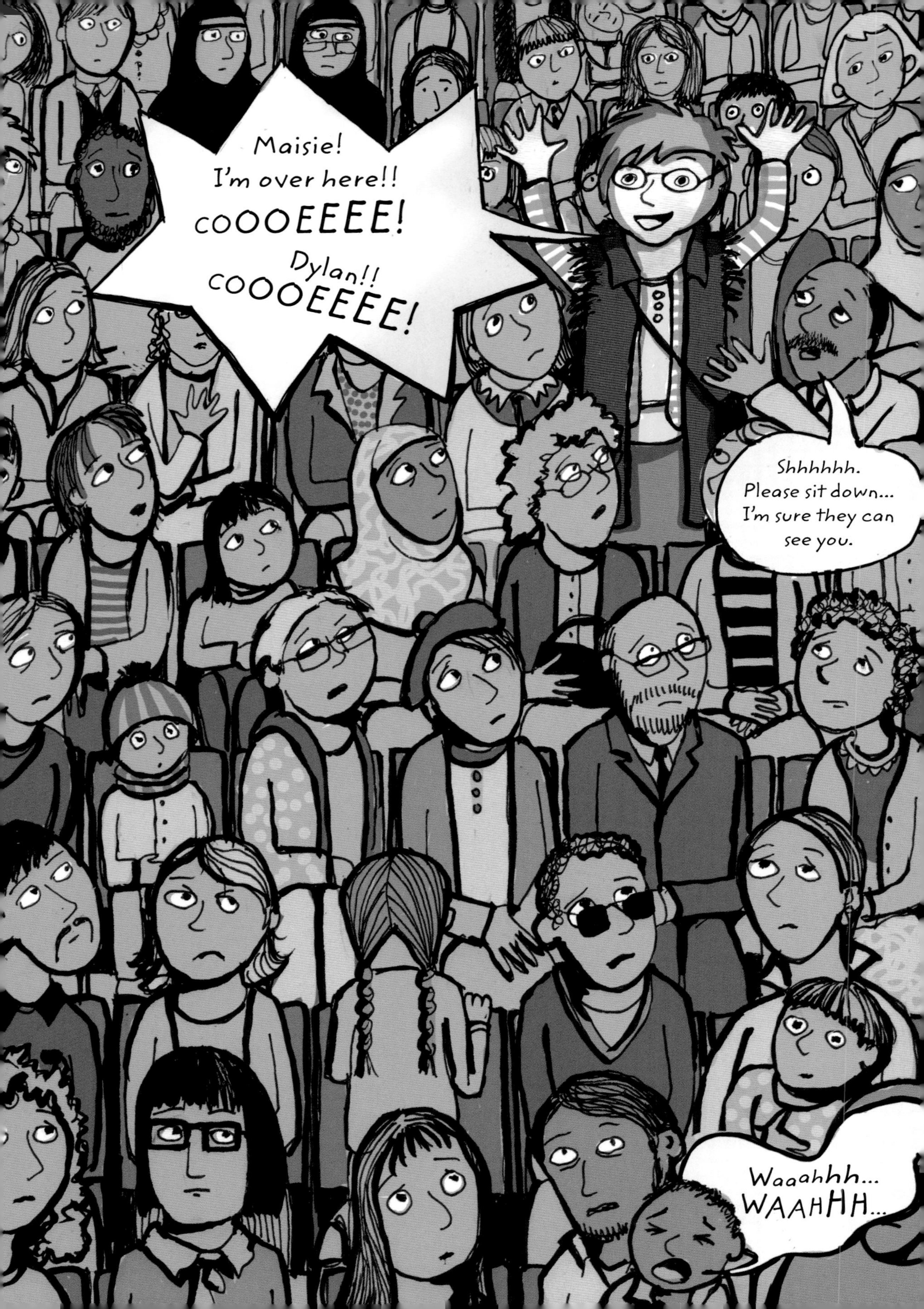
Maisie! I'm over here!! cOOOEEEE! Dylan!! COOOEEEE!
Shhhhhh. Please sit down... I'm sure they can see you.
Waaahhh... WAAHHH...

Once the show was over we were allowed to go home.

We'd better find Granny Moon and take her home.

In the playground outside, Granny Moon was ruffling Liam Williams' hair, even though she didn't know him... and Greg and Michael were making fun of her!

On the walk home, Granny Moon seemed really tired and distracted. She also seemed to have forgotten about Jack... **and even who Jack was!**

When we got back she fell fast asleep on the sofa. Me and Dylan searched the house and the garden, but we couldn't find Jack anywhere!

We eventually found Jack in the spare bedroom.

We let Jack out in the garden and gave him some food. Then we left him cuddled on the sofa with Granny Moon.

That night I couldn't sleep. I worried about Granny Moon and Jack all night... but the next day they were waiting for us after school as usual.

But when we got inside... there was nobody there!

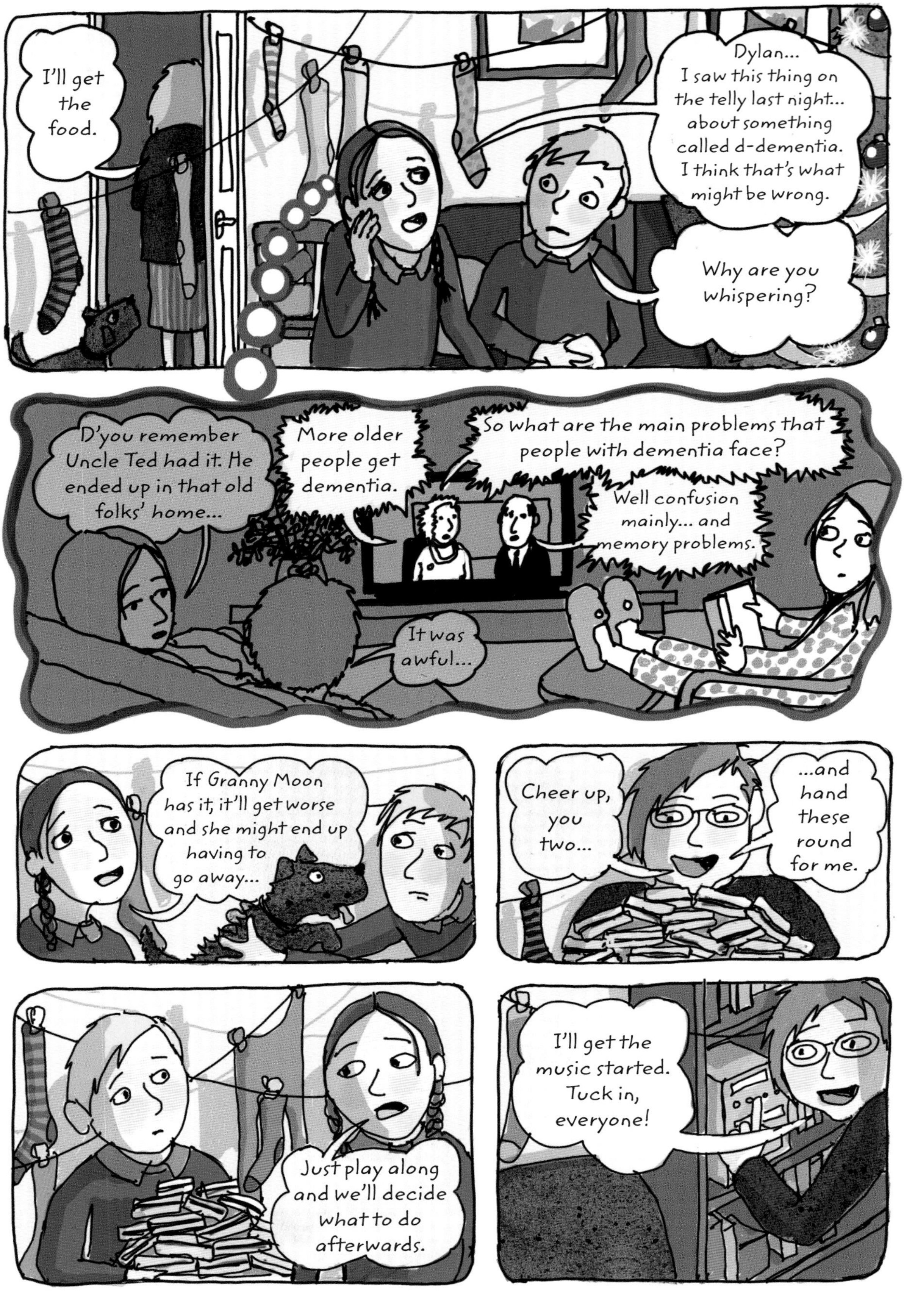

I'll get the food.
Dylan... I saw this thing on the telly last night... about something called d-dementia. I think that's what might be wrong.
Why are you whispering?
D'you remember Uncle Ted had it. He ended up in that old folks' home...
More older people get dementia.
So what are the main problems that people with dementia face?
Well confusion mainly... and memory problems.
It was awful...
If Granny Moon has it, it'll get worse and she might end up having to go away...
Cheer up, you two...
...and hand these round for me.
Just play along and we'll decide what to do afterwards.
I'll get the music started. Tuck in, everyone!

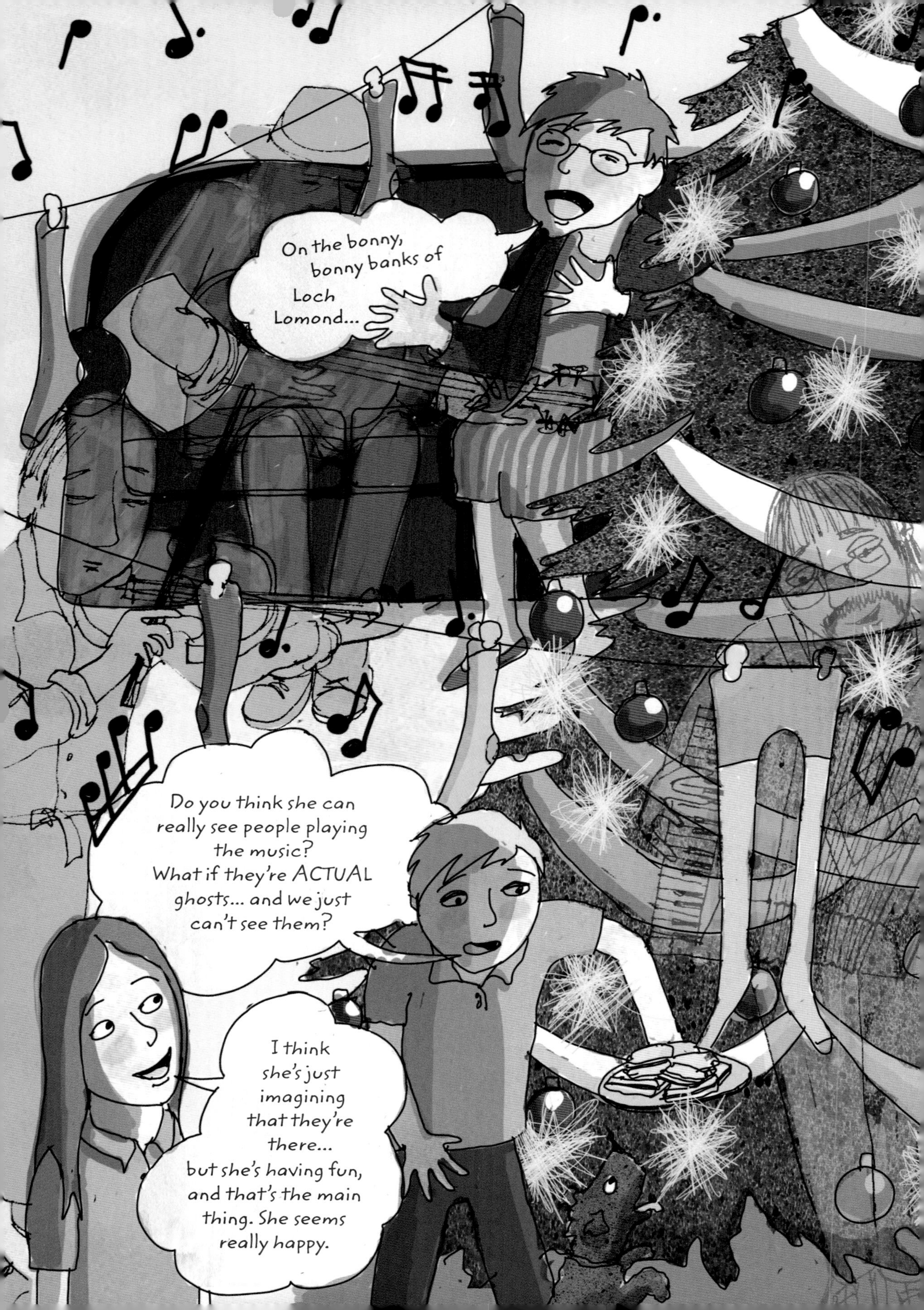
On the bonny, bonny banks of Loch Lomond...
Do you think she can really see people playing the music? What if they're ACTUAL ghosts... and we just can't see them?
I think she's just imagining that they're there... but she's having fun, and that's the main thing. She seems really happy.

All the singing made Granny Moon tired. She and Jack fell fast asleep on the sofa while we tidied up all the uneaten sandwiches.

Shhh. Hopefully she'll have forgotten about the band when she wakes up.

ZZZz

I'll have to put all these in the bin... I'm too full to eat any more...

and I think Jack's had enough too!

Don't tell your parents, will you? I don't want Granny Moon to have to go away...

For the next few days Granny Moon forgot about the imaginary band, and a week later it was Christmas Day. As usual Granny Moon came to our house for dinner. Luckily Mum and Dad didn't seem to notice anything was wrong.

I had friends from Ireland staying. They know how to party... just like the old days.

We're off to see my parents tomorrow... just hope the weather keeps fine.

Angela sang really well at the school concert... but then she's always had a good voice.

You mean Maisie. Yes, I heard it was really good.

The next day we left early to go to Grandma and Grandad's in Scotland for a week. I was so worried about leaving Granny Moon on her own that my stomach ached nearly all the way.

When we arrived it was snowing! We went sledging and made a giant snowman. I played chess with Grandma, and Grandad made chocolate muffins. I forgot about everything else for a while.

On the way back home I began to worry all over again. When we arrived I rushed straight round next door but Granny Moon didn't answer. When I looked through the letter box...

Granny Moon was kneeling on the floor. She was dressed in an old nightie and she looked really, REALLY upset.

It's me, Maisie. Can you let me in?

Oh Maisie... I've been so worried. There's a little girl and she's trapped inside the radiator.

How did she get in there?

She cried all night so I had to stay up just talking to her... what can we do? She's so frightened and lonely.

It'll be OK. We'll sort it out. But first, let's get you dressed and take Jack out for his walk. A bit of fresh air will help...

I managed to calm Granny Moon down and took her out to take her mind off the trapped girl.

He's keen to get to the park today!

I knew that she wasn't playing games and that something must be very wrong. But I was really worried what would happen to her if I told Mum and Dad what was going on. There had to be SOMETHING I could do.

I wished that it was like having a cold and that Granny Moon would just get better, but somehow I knew she wouldn't.

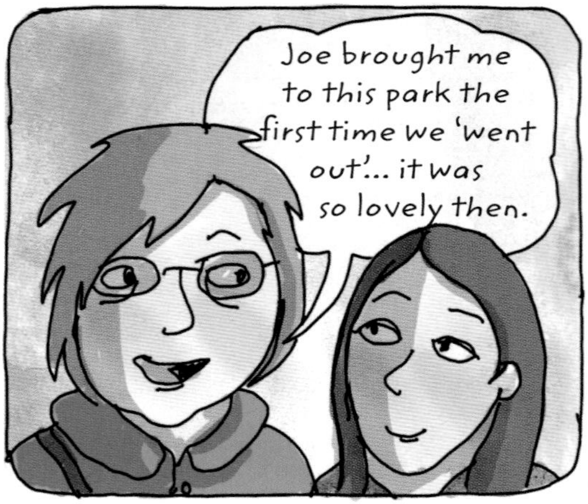
Joe brought me to this park the first time we 'went out'... it was so lovely then.

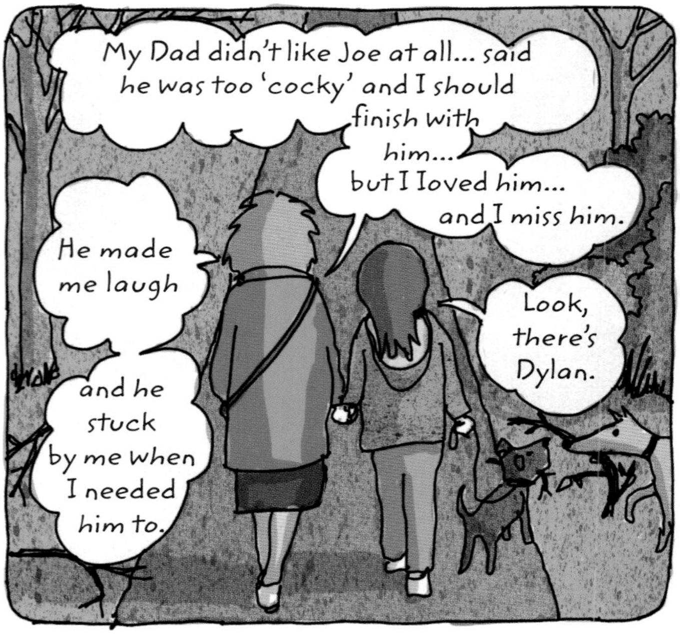
My Dad didn't like Joe at all... said he was too 'cocky' and I should finish with him...
but I loved him... and I miss him.
He made me laugh
and he stuck by me when I needed him to.
Look, there's Dylan.

At the park we saw Dylan and his dad playing football, but Granny Moon didn't seem to recognise them. I hoped Dylan's dad wouldn't notice.

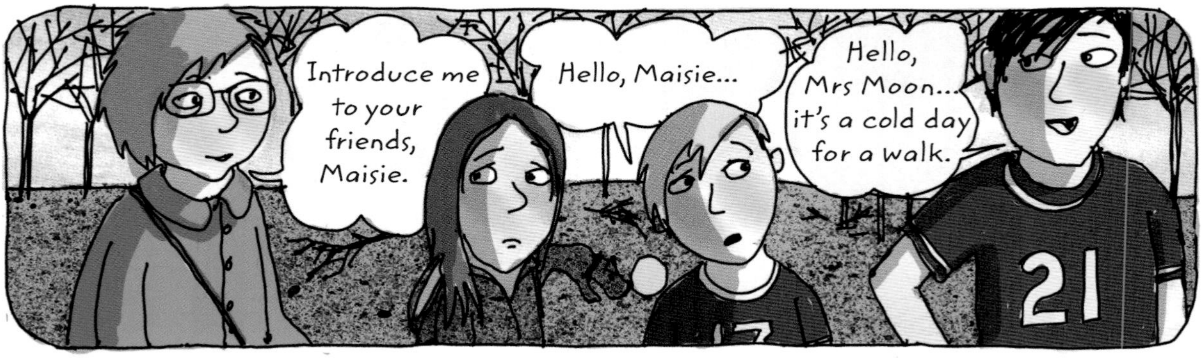
Introduce me to your friends, Maisie.
Hello, Maisie...
Hello, Mrs Moon... it's a cold day for a walk.
21

I hurried away, saying we had to get home, but that upset Granny Moon.

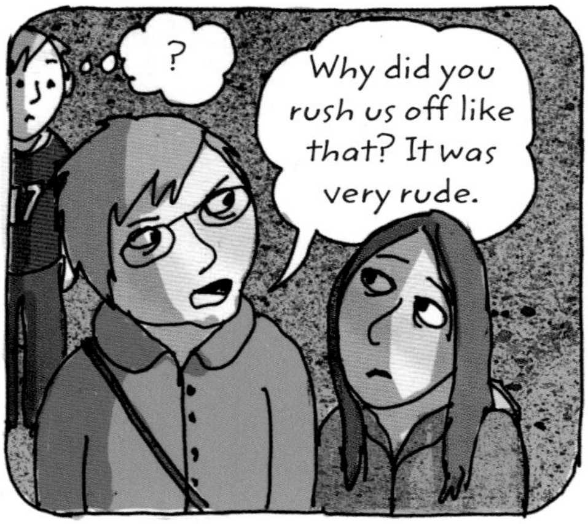
?
Why did you rush us off like that? It was very rude.

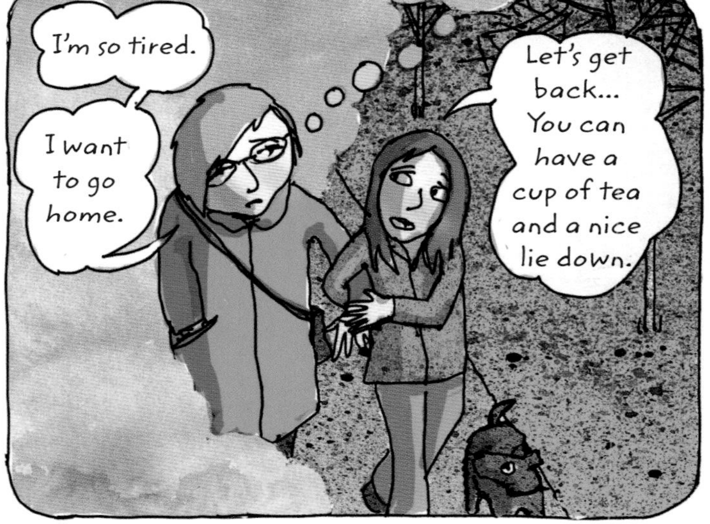
I'm so tired.
I want to go home.
Let's get back... You can have a cup of tea and a nice lie down.

When we got back, Granny Moon and Jack fell fast asleep.

I went home. There was something I needed to do.

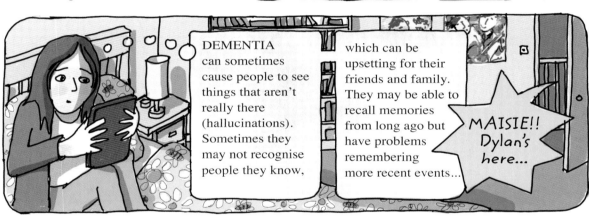

DEMENTIA can sometimes cause people to see things that aren't really there (hallucinations). Sometimes they may not recognise people they know, which can be upsetting for their friends and family. They may be able to recall memories from long ago but have problems remembering more recent events...

MAISIE!! Dylan's here...

Dylan. What's up?

It's my dad. He noticed that Granny Moon was behaving oddly...

I think he might phone your mum about her. He...

he said she was acting weird and maybe she shouldn't look after me any more.

What shall we do?

RING RING!

RING RING!

The next day Mum said she should maybe check up on Mrs Moon.

Luckily, Granny Moon seemed to be her old self when she was talking to Mum... but the next afternoon she was more upset than ever.

Granny Moon fell asleep and I went home... but in the middle of the night I was woken up by really loud bangs that seemed to be coming from Granny Moon's house...

Dad went next door and I sent Dylan a text.

When Dad came back I listened as he told Mum what was going on. They both seemed really worried.

Go back to bed, Maisie. We're going to sort everything out. It'll be OK.

Mum and Dad went downstairs to call Angela and I listened at the bedroom door.

MAISIE'S DEN

Yes hello... is that Angela...? Yes it's Fiona, your mum's next-door-neighbour. Yes. Oh we're very well, thank you... But it's your mum... she's not well... she's been acting a bit strangely... and tonight she's been smashing the radiator in the hall and has been really upset... No, Tom's sorted it out... she's settled now.

No... we'll keep our eye on her until you get here. Yes I agree... she might need to be looked after properly... OK... that'd be great. Let us know when you'll arrive. Bye. Yes, of course... Bye...

I don't know... it's very odd. No, she hasn't done too much damage but the house is in a bit of a mess... Tom says she's got lots of socks hanging up in the lounge and the most enormous Christmas tree... with toilet paper all over it.

I went back to bed and tried to sleep, but I couldn't. I worried that if Angela came, they might decide to send Granny Moon away... and she'd be miserable and scared... and I couldn't bear it.
And I was worried that I'd never see her or Jack again.

The next day was the first day of term. I was really tired and didn't want to wake up.

Come on, Maisie. You'll be late.

You and Dylan will have to walk home on your own today. Mrs Moon's not well.

Do we have to?

Bye, Dad. See you later.

Now be sure to come straight home after school. Bye.

I didn't have a good day at school. I was worried about Granny Moon and about me and Dylan walking home on our own.

We spent all lunch-time talking about what might happen when Angela arrived.

So now Mum and Dad know there's something wrong and they say Angela will have to do something... She's coming to sort it all out.

Maybe she'll come back and live at home again? Granny Moon would like that...

No. Mum says her life's in Australia now. She can't come back. I think she'll put her in a care home and Granny Moon will hate it.

My grandad's in a care home. Dad doesn't really like visiting him though, so we don't go very often.

When school finished, we packed our bags and walked out into the playground where all the parents and grandparents were waiting as usual....

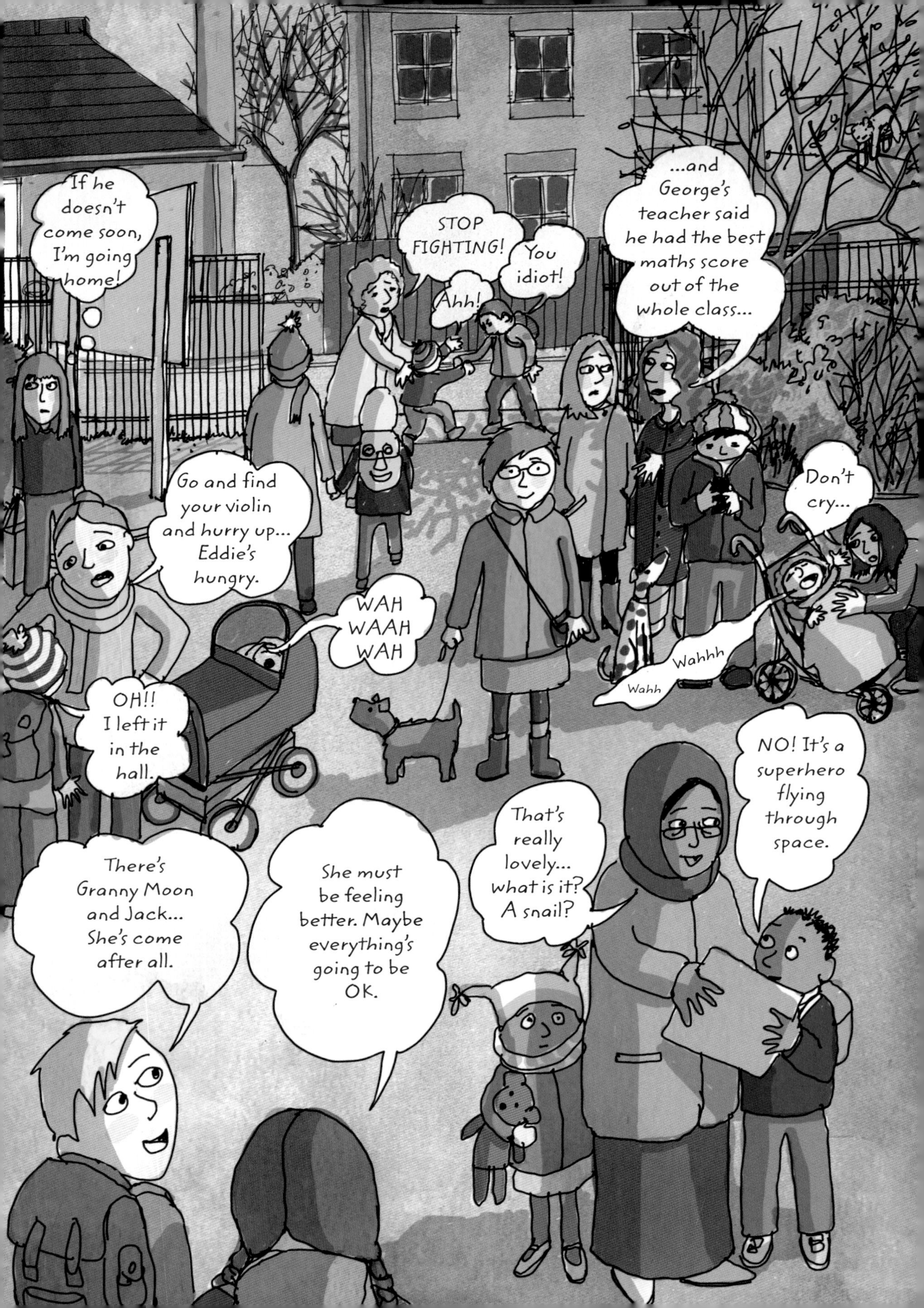

If he doesn't come soon, I'm going home!
STOP FIGHTING!
Ahh!
You idiot!
...and George's teacher said he had the best maths score out of the whole class...
Go and find your violin and hurry up... Eddie's hungry.
Don't cry...
WAH WAAH WAH
Wahhh
Wahh
OH!! I left it in the hall.
NO! It's a superhero flying through space.
That's really lovely... what is it? A snail?
There's Granny Moon and Jack... She's come after all.
She must be feeling better. Maybe everything's going to be OK.

Granny Moon took us to the café on the way home for a treat, and there she bumped into an old friend...

When we noticed how late it was, we said goodbye and set off for home.

It was nearly dark, but as we got to the corner of our street we saw flashing lights. There was a huge fire engine and a police car right outside my house.

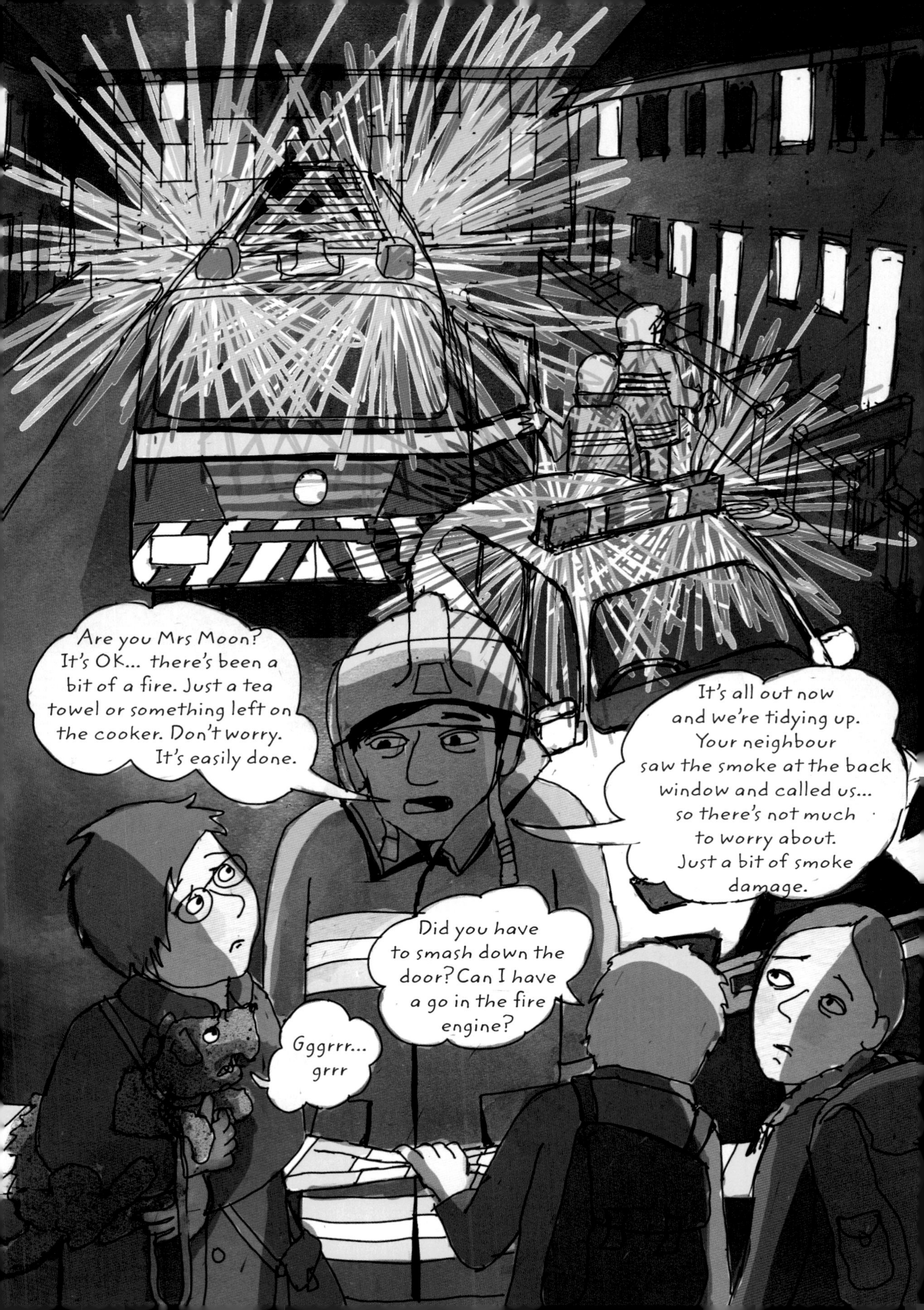
Are you Mrs Moon? It's OK... there's been a bit of a fire. Just a tea towel or something left on the cooker. Don't worry. It's easily done.
It's all out now and we're tidying up. Your neighbour saw the smoke at the back window and called us... so there's not much to worry about. Just a bit of smoke damage.
Did you have to smash down the door? Can I have a go in the fire engine?
Gggrrr... grrr

When we got in, Mum was really angry with us. Dylan got a ride home in the police car but Mum told me to go to my bedroom.

Your dad is out looking for you...

and I told the police officer you were missing.

When I said come straight home, I MEANT come straight home! I've been worried SICK!

The next day we hurried home from school. When we got back, Angela had arrived and was just getting out of a taxi.

Hello, Maisie... Gosh you've grown since I last saw you. How's your mum and dad?

Hello, Angela. They're OK, thanks. Do you want any help with your bags?

Thank you.

That evening when I was doing my homework, she came round to see Mum and Dad...

I didn't realise Mum was so bad. The house is a mess and she's really VERY confused... I'll have to call the doctor and social services in the morning.

It's just hard to know where to start.

Let us know what we can do to help.

I can pop in and check the radiators again...

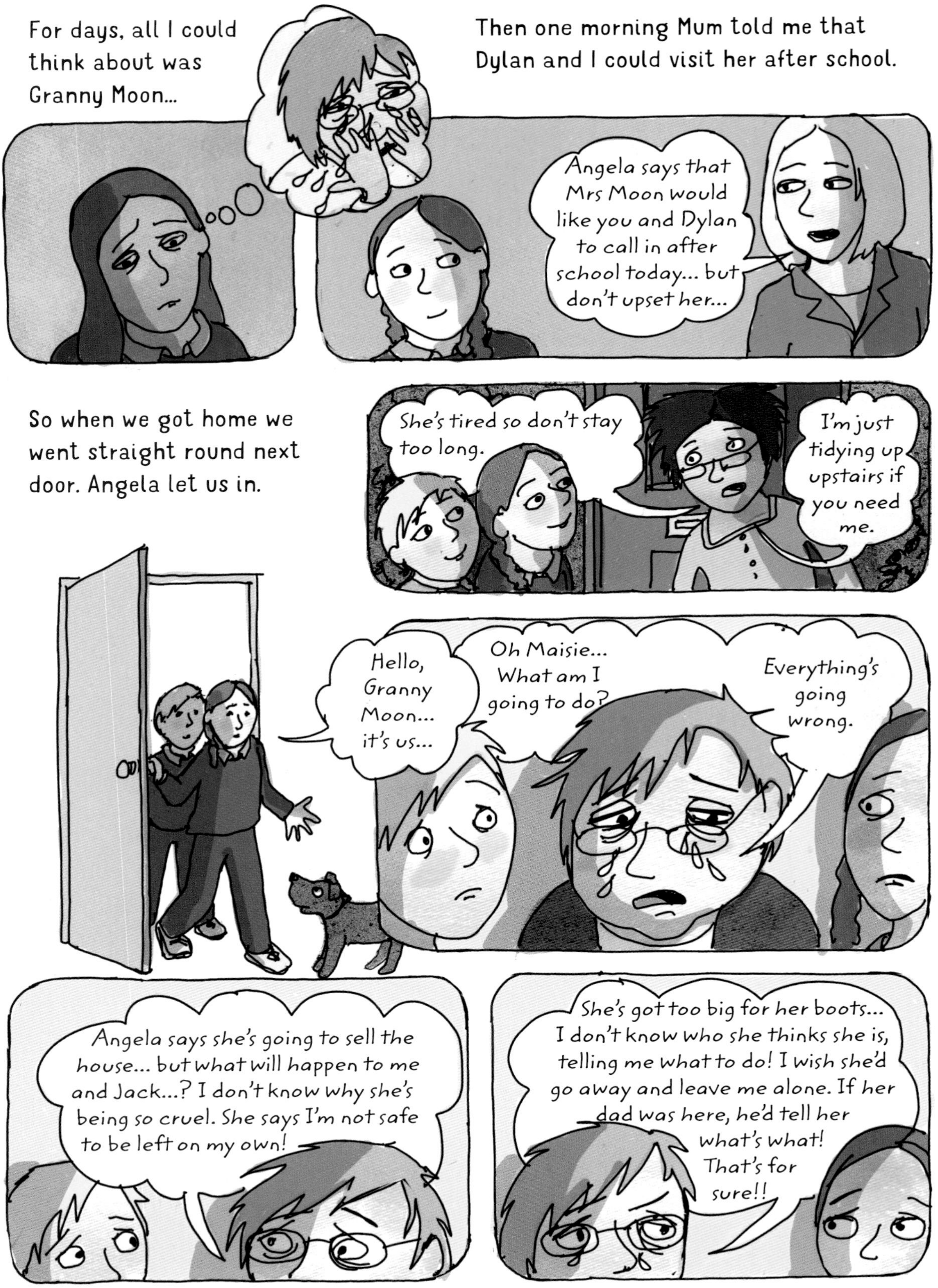
For days, all I could think about was Granny Moon...
Then one morning Mum told me that Dylan and I could visit her after school.
Angela says that Mrs Moon would like you and Dylan to call in after school today... but don't upset her...
So when we got home we went straight round next door. Angela let us in.
She's tired so don't stay too long.
I'm just tidying up upstairs if you need me.
Hello, Granny Moon... it's us...
Oh Maisie... What am I going to do?
Everything's going wrong.
Angela says she's going to sell the house... but what will happen to me and Jack...? I don't know why she's being so cruel. She says I'm not safe to be left on my own!
She's got too big for her boots... I don't know who she thinks she is, telling me what to do! I wish she'd go away and leave me alone. If her dad was here, he'd tell her what's what! That's for sure!!

Me and Dylan did our best to cheer Granny Moon up.

I've made us all my special strawberry milkshake...

Now we could watch the antiques programme... or that quiz with the comedian and his dog...

Yes. Let's watch that... he's really funny, and the dog's just like Jack.

Maybe we could teach Jack to do that?

Oooh... he's so funny...

Jack wouldn't sit still enough.

We'd better go now she's asleep... careful not to wake her...

ZZZZ
ZZZZ
ZZZ
ZZ

As we left, there was a sound of soft crying from upstairs. Angela came down the stairs, wiping her eyes...

Angela... we're off now!

Sob... sob...

What's that noise?

OK... sniff... thanks for coming... sniff... tell your mum I'll call in later, Maisie... Bye, Dylan... Bye.

Bye then.

Outside there was a man putting up a signboard.

Hello, kids... cheer up... It might never happen! Ha, ha, ha...

That night I was doing my homework when Angela called round again to see Mum and Dad.

I was going to take Mum to see this nice care home... but she refused to go and look at it, and now she won't talk to me... They say I need to decide this week! ...sniff... I just don't know what to do...

But why can't we look after her? I see her all the time anyway and she feels at home here. She could still sleep at her house and...

MAISIE! You don't understand... This is not for you to worry about.

But I wasn't going to stay silent. I wasn't going to let them send Granny Moon away without trying to help them understand. I told Angela everything that had happened.

I love Granny Moon and she loves us... and we've all been so happy. Whenever we're miserable she cheers us up, and if we're hurt or a bit worried, she can always make things better. She's our best friend and I love her more than ever now, because she needs our help.

She's only been trying to rescue the frightened little girl that she thinks is trapped in the radiator... I think she must feel just like that scared little girl... and she's trying so hard to make sense of the world, and she just doesn't understand it any more...

And then I burst into tears!!

Don't cry... you just need a good night's sleep.

Come on... Things always seem better in the morning...

Sometimes we have to make difficult decisions... and it might be hard to understand... don't worry.

One evening a few days later, me and Dylan were working on our penguins project when Angela came round.

This is a really good website. It says there are 595,000 Emperor penguins in Antarctica.

Oh, hello, Angela. Come in... are things OK?

I've been frantically busy trying to get things sorted out before I go back next week... and I've just come to tell you what I've arranged. I hope you won't be too upset.

Then Angela took us COMPLETELY by suprise!

Mum and I have agreed that she will come back to Australia to live with me... she's quite excited about it.

I know you'll miss her, Maisie, and she'll miss you all... but what you said made me realise that I want the chance to show her Australia and spend some time with her... and I want Nathan to have fun with his Grandma and get to know her, like you two know her. She's always liked an adventure and this will be her chance for one more big adventure... I know there'll be problems, but we'll manage... Are you both OK with that plan?

Oh thank you. She'll LOVE it... I'm SO glad.

From then on things happened very quickly. We went shopping and started packing.

My favourite... shopping for summer dresses.

I think you'll need a sun hat too. It'll stop you getting sunburned.

It's gone dark! Hee Hee Hee!

50%

It might be in the Sale but I think that one's a bit TOO big!!

I'll never get all these new clothes into this bag... it won't close.

There was so much stuff to take and there was lots to get rid of too.

These should sell well... they're real antiques!

But what about Jack?

We packed boxes with things to take to the charity shops. But then at the last minute, we thought of a problem.

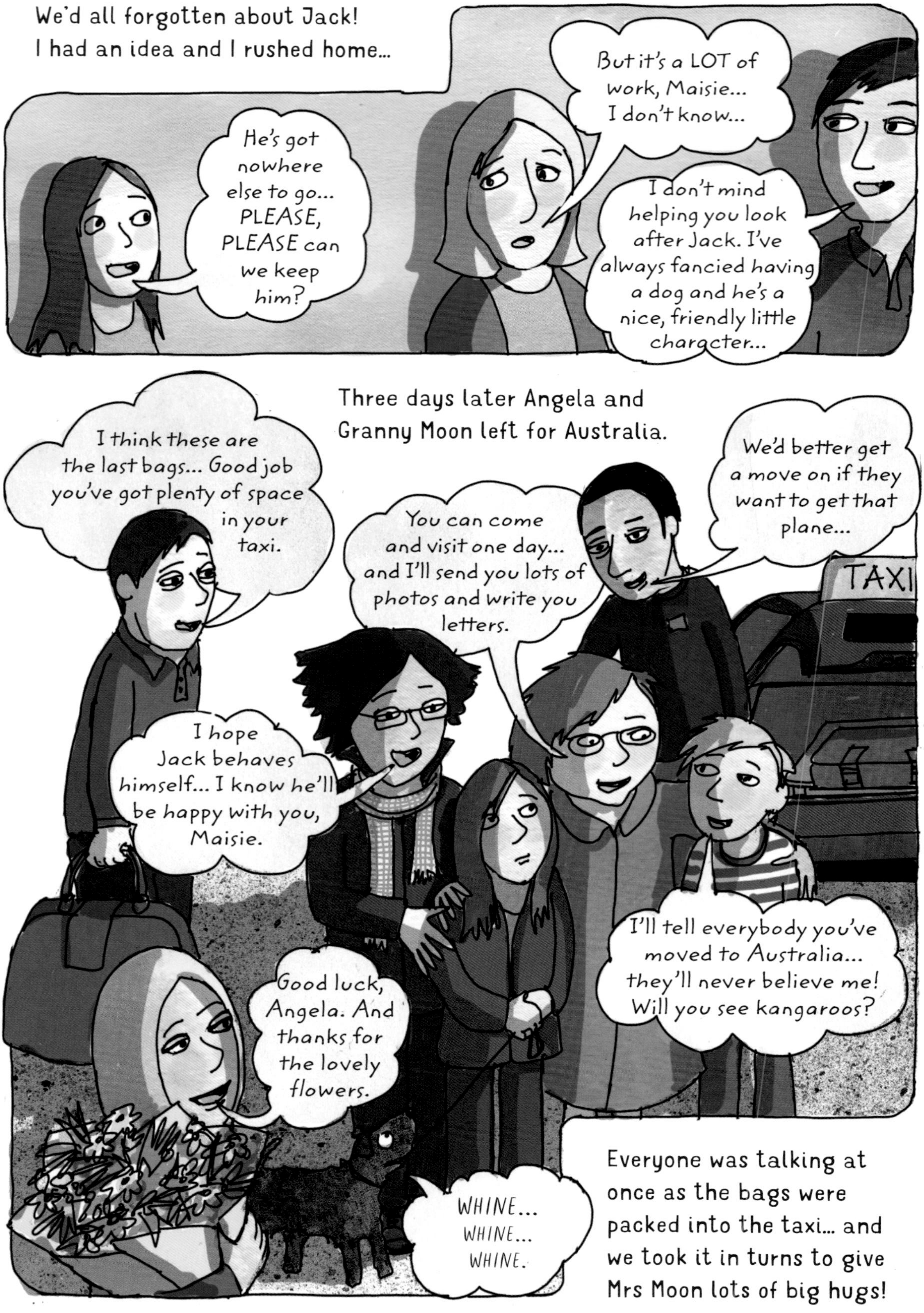
We'd all forgotten about Jack!
I had an idea and I rushed home...
He's got nowhere else to go... PLEASE, PLEASE can we keep him?
But it's a LOT of work, Maisie... I don't know...
I don't mind helping you look after Jack. I've always fancied having a dog and he's a nice, friendly little character...
Three days later Angela and Granny Moon left for Australia.
I think these are the last bags... Good job you've got plenty of space in your taxi.
You can come and visit one day... and I'll send you lots of photos and write you letters.
We'd better get a move on if they want to get that plane...
TAXI
I hope Jack behaves himself... I know he'll be happy with you, Maisie.
I'll tell everybody you've moved to Australia... they'll never believe me! Will you see kangaroos?
Good luck, Angela. And thanks for the lovely flowers.
WHINE... WHINE... WHINE.
Everyone was talking at once as the bags were packed into the taxi... and we took it in turns to give Mrs Moon lots of big hugs!

I felt really, really sad as I watched the taxi drive away... it was like a part of me was being lost for ever.

Come on, you two. Let's take Jack for a walk by the canal...

Is he always this noisy? It's a good job he's on his lead or he'd be in the canal!

He used to jump in the lake at the park. He just hates ducks!

STOP, JACK!

WOOF... WOOF...

I miss Granny Moon a lot. I talk to Jack about all the good times we had together. Dylan says he's only a dog – but I know he understands.

Do you know someone with dementia?

If you do, you'll know that, like Mrs Moon, their condition can change from day to day – sometimes they're quite all right, sometimes confused, angry or upset. That can be hard to live with, and also for their friends, relatives and carers to cope with.

Lots of families have a relative with dementia who may need help looking after themselves. Fortunately, help and support are available. Listed below are some of the organisations set up to help people with dementia, and their families and carers:

The Alzheimer's Society
www.alzheimers.org.uk
www.alz.org (US)

Dementia Australia
www.dementia.org.au

Dementia Adventure (UK)
Holidays for people with dementia
www.dementiaadventure.co.uk

Pictures to Share C.I.C.
Picture books for people with later stage dementia
www.picturestoshare.co.uk

Innovations in Dementia (UK)
Helping people with dementia stay in control of their lives
www.innovationsindementia.org.uk

Dementia friends (UK)
Teaching everyone how they can help people with dementia
www.dementiafriends.org.uk

The Carers Trust
www.carers.org/about-us/about-young-carers